The Mitten Tree

CANDACE CHRISTIANSEN

ILLUSTRATED BY ELAINE GREENSTEIN

FULCRUM
GOLDEN, COLORADO

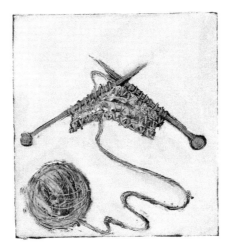

For Kaulini and her mom and dad
—C. C.

For Carl, Alicia, Carl Jr., and Noah Keller
—E. G.

At the end of a long lane, in a tidy little house, old Sarah lived alone. Her children had grown up and moved away, but Sarah still remembered the mornings when she walked with them to the blue spruce tree where they waited for the school bus. Now each morning she opened her shutters and watched for new children to arrive.

Every chilly morning Sarah pulled on her warm coat and started down the lane. As she walked past the children on her way to the mailbox, she wished they would smile or wave. But they never did. The children didn't even seem to notice her. Still, when she saw them she couldn't help but smile.

One winter morning after the first snow had fallen, all the children were making snowmen and throwing snowballs. All except for one little boy in a blue cap and coat. Even his boots were a dark shade of blue.

He stood away from the others with his hands sunk deep in his pockets.

When the school bus arrived, he lingered behind and was last in line. As Sarah watched the little boy climb into the bus, she could see one thing—he had no mittens.

All that day Sarah couldn't stop worrying about the little boy with no mittens. Late in the afternoon, as the sky grew dark, Sarah dug through the basket of yarn scraps she had saved for many years. She found her needles and four shades of blue wool. Then, Sarah began to knit.

Sarah worked late into the night. When the sun began to rise, she hurried to the bus stop and hung the mittens on the old blue spruce tree. From behind the hedge, Sarah watched.

The little boy was the first to arrive. He saw the mittens. He reached up and tried them on. They fit. With a big smile, he made a perfect snowball and threw it high into the winter sky.

Soon a little girl in a red coat arrived. Her mittens didn't match. That night Sarah knitted with red yarn.

Every day now as Sarah went to the mailbox, she watched for children without mittens. Then she would hurry home and knit. Early in the morning, she would hang the new mittens on the tree. The children loved the game. Each day they would search under every branch and bough for another pair of mittens.

Once or twice, Sarah thought that the boy with the blue mittens had seen her, but he always looked away.

Night after night, Sarah knitted mittens in every color. Some had stripes, some had hearts, some even had little snowflakes all over them.

Somehow, even though she had never spoken to the children, Sarah felt that they had become her new family.

On the last day before winter vacation, Sarah awakened before dawn. She took the empty basket that had once held her yarn and filled it to the brim with mittens. Out the door and down the steps she headed. When she got to the blue spruce tree, she hung mittens on every branch.

The boy with the blue mittens was the first to arrive.
He stood very still and waited for the others. In fact,
all the children stood very still for a few minutes looking
at the mysterious, beautiful mitten tree.

When they boarded the bus, each child now wore
a new pair of mittens.

Sarah watched as, one by one, their faces appeared
in the bus windows. Still no one looked her way as she
started home.

But Sarah's heart was full. It was as full as when the sounds of her own children had filled her house.

As Sarah neared her porch and climbed the steps, she saw something waiting for her. There in the corner was a basket woven with thick brown vines and decorated with a large white bow. In it were balls and balls of beautiful, colorful yarn.

To this day, Sarah knits mittens for all the children in her town. Every time her basket is empty, a new full one appears.

Sarah doesn't know who the yarn is from. The children still don't know who the mittens are from.

But someone must …

Library of Congress Cataloging-in-Publication Data
Christiansen, Candace.
    The mitten tree / Candace Christiansen ; illustrated by Elaine Greenstein.
        p.   cm.
    Summary: Old Sarah knits mittens for all the children waiting for the school bus and hangs them on the blue spruce tree at the bus stop.
    ISBN 978-1-55591-349-6 (hardcover)
    ISBN 978-1-55591-733-3 (paperback)
    [1. Mittens—Fiction. 2. Neighborliness—Fiction.]
I. Greenstein, Elaine, ill.   II. Title.
PZ7.C45287Mi   1997
[E]—dc21   96-53358
                                                                    CIP
                                                                    AC

Printed in the United States
0 9 8 7 6 5

Fulcrum Publishing
4690 Table Mountain Dr., Ste. 100
Golden, Colorado 80403
800-992-2908 • 303-277-1623
www.fulcrumbooks.com